LEVEL 2 READER

FLASH FORWARD FAIRY*TALES

Cinderella IN THE City

A retelling by Cari Meister

Illustrated by Erica-Jane Waters

SCHOLASTIC INC

For John (my prince charming) and Edwin
(a prince charming in training) – C.M.

For Nick and Sienna – E.J.W.

ISBN 978-0-545-56568-4

Text copyright © 2014 by Cari Meister.
Illustrations copyright © 2014 by Erica-Jane Waters.
All rights reserved. Published by Scholastic Inc.
SCHOLASTIC and associated logos are trademarks and/or registered trademarks of Scholastic Inc.

12 11 10 9 8 7 6 5 4 3   14 15 16 17 18 19/0

Printed in the U.S.A.   40
First printing, May 2014

Designed by Liz Herzog

Once upon a time, a girl named Cinderella lived with her cruel stepmother and two ugly stepsisters. They would not let her attend the royal ball.

But a fairy godmother used magic to turn Cinderella into a princess for one night.

Cinderella went to the ball, fell in love with a prince, and danced until the magic ran out at midnight. Then she ran away, leaving behind one glass slipper. The prince tried the slipper on every girl in the kingdom, looking for his true love. . . .

But that was then. Flash forward to TODAY . . .

Early one morning, Cindy got a text from her stepmom, Helen.

TO: Cindy

FROM: Helen

Get me a double mocha with whipped cream. Pronto!

Cindy got dressed and jumped on her skateboard.

On the way to the café, Cindy spotted a poster.

"I MUST enter that contest!" she said.

She practiced her dance moves all the way to the coffee shop.

When Cindy got home, Helen and her stepsisters kept her so busy that she forgot all about the contest.

"Wash my yoga pants," said Helen.

"Do my homework," said Fay.

"Fix my hair," said May.

Just then, the doorbell rang. It was the doorman. He presented a letter sealed with a sticker.

"It's an invite from Prince Edwin to the dance contest tomorrow night," said Fay.

"But we don't even dance," said May.

"You do now!" said Helen. "Get off the couch. I'll teach you."

They weren't very good. In fact, they were very, very bad.

"I can dance," Cinderella said. "May I go?"

"No," said Helen. "You have too many chores to do."

Cindy's heart sank.

But after everyone went to bed, Cindy couldn't help practicing her best moves.

The next afternoon, the girls were in a tizzy.

"Cinderella," said May. "Fix my hair!"

"No!" said Fay. "Fix MY hair!"

Cindy fixed them both. "Perfect!" she said.

The silly girls agreed. They flopped down the hall with their mother.

"I hear Prince Ed is handsome," said May.

"Stay away from him," said Fay. "He's mine!"

Cinderella closed the door and sighed.

"I wish I could show off my moves," she said.

"You can!" said a voice.

"Who said that?" asked Cinderella.

"Your fairy godmother!" said the glittering woman who suddenly appeared before her.

"I must be dreaming," said Cindy.

"No," said the fairy. "You're not. But we don't have much time. You have a prince to meet!"

And with a flash of the fairy's wand,
Cindy's outfit went from drab to fab!

"Catch!" The fairy threw her a set of keys.

Cindy looked out the window at the scooter parked below. It was awesome!

"One last thing," the fairy called as
Cindy rushed out the door. "The magic
runs out at midnight. Well, everything but
the shoes. Can't seem to figure those out."

Cindy stepped into the ballroom just as Fay and May were taking their turn on the dance floor with Prince Ed.

It didn't go well.

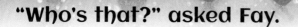

"Who's that?" asked Fay.

"Her shoes are awesome!" cried May.

Prince Ed leaped over to Cindy. "Care to dance?" he asked.

"I'd love to," Cindy said.

Prince Ed and Cinderella twirled and tangoed and wiggled and waltzed all night.

"We have a winner!" cried the judges.

"Who *are* you?" asked Prince Ed.

Cindy was about to take off her mask when—

BEEP! BEEP! BEEP!

Her cell-phone alarm went off.

"It's midnight!" Cindy gasped.

She rushed from the ballroom, leaving one magical shoe behind.

The next morning, Prince Ed was on the news.

"Will the dancer who wore this shoe last night please come to the ballroom to claim it?"

"Let's go!" said Helen.

"It's not our shoe," said May.

"Says who?" said Fay.

In the ballroom, hundreds of girls lined up to try on the glass slipper.

Fay's foot was too fat.

May's foot was too long.

The prince sighed. "The dancer of my dreams must not be here," he said.

"May I try?" asked Cinderella. She stepped forward, already wearing the other slipper.

Prince Edwin slipped the second shoe on. It fit perfectly.

"Will you be my partner at the Royal Dance Academy?" he asked.

"Absolutely!" said Cindy.

Cindy grabbed Prince Edwin's hand as a band began to play. They strutted and swayed and twisted and two-stepped.

And then they danced off to begin their new life together at the Royal Dance Academy.